MATHS Workbook

Level 6

MOONSTONE

Published in Moonstone
by Rupa Publications India Pvt. Ltd 2022
7/16, Ansari Road, Daryaganj
New Delhi 110002

Sales centres:
Allahabad Bengaluru Chennai
Hyderabad Jaipur Kathmandu
Kolkata Mumbai

ISBN: 978-93-5520-714-2

First impression 2022

10 9 8 7 6 5 4 3 2 1

Contents

Numbers

1. Mark the commas to segregate periods and write the number names for the following.

(a) 7848305 = ____________________

(b) 20770999 = ____________________

(c) 8965130 = ____________________

(d) 7349056 = ____________________

(e) 41376008 = ____________________

2. Arrange the following numbers in the ascending order.

(a) 7,22,346 6,56,532 9,06,490 1,56,530

____

(b) 7,81,045 59,28,640 9,99,999 80,009

____

3. Arrange the following numbers in the descending order.

(a) 24,88,642 83,12,756 6,84,219 79,999

____

(b) 5,16,389 6,53,891 1,85,963 9,83,651

____

4. Write the following numbers in the expanded form.

(a) 8476535 = ______________________

(b) 4001807 = ______________________

(c) 27729372 = ______________________

(d) 76960045 = ______________________

(e) 14677620 = ______________________

5. Write the numerals for the following.

(a) Three crore fifty six lakh three hundred seventy three ____________

(b) Forty nine lakh thirty two thousand seven hundred fifty ____________

(c) Sixty five crore ninety four lakh nine hundred nine ____________

(d) Thirteen crore five lakh seventy eight ____________

(e) Seventy lakh fifty nine thousand twelve ____________

6. Write the next two numbers for the patterns given below.

(a) 7,63,148 7,65,148 7,67,148 ____________ ____________

(b) 40,10,100 40,20,200 40,30,300 ____________ ____________

(c) 17,11,497 27,11,497 37,11,497 ____________ ____________

(d) 8,50,621 8,51,631 8,52,641 ____________ ____________

(e) 53,285 53,785 54,285 ____________ ____________

7. Round off the following numbers to the nearest thousand.

(a) 4639 ____________ (b) 19065 ____________

(c) 23555 ____________ (d) 36429 ____________

(e) 19862 ____________ (f) 99840 ____________

(g) 183246 ____________ (h) 259340 ____________

8. Estimate the answer of the following to the nearest thousand.

(a) 4728 + 1639 + 2110 + 2397

Estimated answer = ____________

Actual answer = ____________

(b) 37180 + 43684 + 4986 + 3729

Estimated answer = ____________

Actual answer = ____________

(c) 76860 – 61429 + 19364

Estimated answer = ____________

Actual answer = ____________

(d) 57 × 260

Estimated product = ____________

Actual product = ____________

(e) 48600 ÷ 12

Estimated quotient = ______________

Actual quotient = ______________

(f) 276000 ÷ 60

Estimated quotient = ______________

Actual quotient = ______________

(g) 270 × 640

Estimated product = ______________

Actual product = ______________

9. Round off the following numbers to the nearest 100.

(a) 375 ______________ (b) 498 ______________

(c) 550 ______________ (d) 1060 ______________

(e) 241 ______________ (f) 1105 ______________

(g) 823 ______________ (h) 964 ______________

10. Write the following as Hindu-Arabic numerals.

(a) MDCLIV __________ (b) CLVII __________

(c) XXXIV + XL __________ (d) XL + XXVIII __________

(e) MD – CCL __________ (f) CMLX __________

(g) DCCVI __________ (h) MCV __________

11. Answer the following questions.

(a) A lady earns \$652 every month. Estimate the amount of money earned by her in two years.

Answer: ____________________

(b) Mohan has 3264 red balls, 6102 blue balls and 4729 yellow balls. Find the estimated number of balls by rounding off the numbers to the nearest thousand.

Answer: ____________________

(c) There are 459 pages in a book. If each page has 1600 words, estimate the total number of words by rounding off to the nearest hundred.

Answer: ____________________

(d) In an election, the winning party gets, 3,41,800 more votes than the losing party. If the losing party gets 18,43,200 votes, how many votes did the winning party get?

Answer: ____________________

Number Operations

1. Simplify the following.

(a) 80000 – 64239 = __________ (b) 2064 ÷ 3 = __________

(c) 78 × 232 = __________ (d) 467892 + 96278 = __________

(e) 13431 ÷ 11 = __________ (f) 625 × 55 = __________

(g) 7867049 – 775600 = __________ (h) 69200 ÷ 16 = __________

(i) 555623 + 124089 = __________ (j) 111 × 467 = __________

2. Solve the following numerical expressions.

(a) 29 + 14 – 17 × 0 = __________

(b) 49 ÷ 7 – 6 ÷ 2 + 2 = __________

(c) 684 ÷ 9 × 4 – 199 = __________

(d) 810 + 162 ÷ 3 – 64 = __________

3. Answer the following.

(a) The value of 7 + (6 × 8) is __________.

(b) We use __________ rule to simplify numerical expressions which have more than one operation.

(c) The value of 8 × (2 + 2) – 16 is __________ .

(d) The value of 11 + 15 – (24 ÷ 6) × 3 is __________ .

Fractions

1. Reduce the fractions to their lowest form.

a. $\frac{70}{84} = \square$

b. $3\frac{2}{6} = \square$

c. $\frac{52}{65} = \square$

d. $\frac{45}{54} = \square$

e. $\frac{63}{84} = \square$

f. $\frac{16}{50} = \square$

2. Write any three equivalent fractions for the following.

a. $\frac{5}{13} = \square$

b. $\frac{4}{7} = \square$

c. $\frac{9}{18} = \square$

d. $\frac{5}{8} = \square$

e. $\frac{2}{11} = \square$

f. $\frac{7}{9} = \square$

3. Fill in the blanks.

a. $\frac{3}{11} = \frac{24}{\square} = \frac{\square}{55} = \frac{51}{\square} = \frac{\square}{121}$

b. $\frac{6}{13} = \frac{36}{\square} = \frac{54}{\square} = \frac{\square}{143} = \frac{78}{\square}$

c. $\frac{5}{8} = \frac{55}{\square} = \frac{\square}{96} = \frac{\square}{120} = \frac{100}{\square}$

d. $\frac{2}{9} = \frac{24}{\square} = \frac{\square}{81} = \frac{56}{\square} = \frac{\square}{108}$

e. $\frac{4}{7} = \frac{60}{\square} = \frac{72}{\square} = \frac{\square}{91} = \frac{\square}{700}$

4. Compare the fractions using > , < or =.

a. $\frac{2}{8}$ ☐ $\frac{3}{12}$

b. $\frac{7}{8}$ ☐ $\frac{1}{3}$

c. $\frac{6}{11}$ ☐ $\frac{9}{11}$

d. $\frac{8}{13}$ ☐ $\frac{8}{11}$

e. $\frac{3}{14}$ ☐ $\frac{2}{7}$

f. $\frac{4}{9}$ ☐ $\frac{5}{12}$

g. $\frac{2}{5}$ ☐ $\frac{3}{7}$

h. $\frac{7}{15}$ ☐ $\frac{5}{9}$

5. Arrange the following in the ascending order.

a. $\frac{3}{7}, \frac{9}{7}, \frac{1}{7}, \frac{4}{14}, \frac{6}{7}$ ☐

b. $\frac{4}{7}, \frac{1}{9}, \frac{3}{5}, \frac{4}{5}, \frac{2}{7}$ ☐

c. $\frac{3}{12}, \frac{4}{12}, \frac{6}{12}, \frac{2}{12}$ ☐

d. $\frac{5}{8}, \frac{8}{9}, \frac{2}{3}, \frac{3}{4}$ ☐

6. Arrange the following in the descending order.

a. $\frac{4}{9}$, $\frac{1}{8}$, $\frac{3}{6}$, $\frac{1}{3}$

b. $\frac{2}{11}$, $\frac{5}{11}$, $\frac{9}{11}$, $\frac{15}{11}$, $\frac{7}{11}$

c. $\frac{3}{13}$, $\frac{6}{15}$, $\frac{1}{5}$, $\frac{8}{13}$

d. $\frac{1}{2}$, $\frac{2}{3}$, $\frac{1}{4}$, $\frac{5}{6}$

7. Solve the following and reduce the answers to their simplest form.

a. $\frac{3}{7} + \frac{6}{13} + \frac{5}{7}$

b. $2\frac{4}{5} + 3\frac{1}{9}$

c. $\frac{7}{12} - \frac{1}{4}$

d. $8 - \left(\frac{2}{5} + \frac{2}{3} + 1\frac{2}{3}\right)$

e. $2\frac{1}{6} + 5\frac{1}{2} - \frac{7}{16}$

f. $\frac{4}{9} + \frac{3}{5} - \frac{1}{3}$

8. Fill in the blanks.

(a) A fraction with 1 as its numerator is called a __________ fraction.

(b) Fractions with the same denominators are called __________ fractions.

(c) $\frac{2}{9}$ is the __________ of fraction $\frac{9}{2}$.

(d) The other way to write the fraction $4\frac{7}{8}$ is __________.

(e) Fractions with different denominators are called __________ fractions.

(f) An equivalent fraction of $\frac{3}{17}$ is __________ .

(g) The lowest form of the fraction $\frac{21}{84}$ is __________.

9. Read the following word problems and find their answers.

(a) A piece of length $3\frac{1}{4}$ m was cut out from a 7 m long rope. How much rope is left? __________

(b) For a recipe, a lady needs 1 $\frac{3}{5}$ cups of flour, $\frac{2}{5}$ cup sugar and 1 cup of milk. How many cups of ingredients does she need in all? __________

(c) A boy read $\frac{2}{7}$ of a book on day 1 and rest on day 2. If there are 343 pages in the book, how many pages did he read on day 2? __________

(d) A courier contains three items weighing $3\frac{1}{4}$ grams, $2\frac{3}{8}$ grams and $10\frac{4}{5}$ grams respectively. What is the total weight of the courier? __________

(e) The length of the side of a square-shaped park is $\frac{3}{5}$ m. If Tiya takes 4 rounds of the park, how much distance was walked by her? __________

(f) A vendor prepared 10 litres of lemonade out of which $3\frac{1}{4}$ litres was sold and $1\frac{1}{4}$ litres was spilled on the floor. How much lemonade is still left?

____

Decimals

1. Solve the following decimal problems.

(a) $0.4 \times (0.1 \times 15)$

(b) $15.6 + (2.1 - 1.8)$

(c) $4.8 + (5.6 \div 7)$

(d) $8.8 + (0.25 \times 1.2)$

(e) $(0.1 \times 0.2) + (14 \times 0.5)$

(f) $1.35 \times (0.2 + 0.3)$

(g) $2.5 \div (6.6 + 3.4)$

(h) $7.5 - (2.4 \times 0.2)$

(i) $9.54 - (0.9 \times 0.6)$

(j) $(4.05 - 2.05) \div 0.2$

2. Identify and write the place value of 5 in the following.

(a) 164.058 = ____________________

(b) 357.081 = ____________________

(c) 83.105 = ____________________

(d) 99.526 = ____________________

3. Fill in the missing numbers to complete the equation.

(a) $8.4 \div 0.2 + \square = 40.5 + 2.8$

(b) $0.08 \times (0.8) + 2.5 = 3.5 - \square$

(c) $(0.2)^2 + \square = 0.4 + (0.4)^2$

(d) $(1.4 - 0.7) + (4)^2 = (5)^2 - \square$

(e) $(0.84 \times 0.5) = (0.6 - 0.25) + \square$

(f) $(4.8 + 0.8) \div 7 = \square - 0.2$

(g) $(0.05 + 0.20) \times \square = 0.75 + 0.25$

4. Solve the following word problems.

(a) A rope measuring 76.8 m was divided into 12 equal pieces. What will be the length of 7 such pieces of rope?

Answer: ____________________

(b) A lady bought 8 pairs of gloves for $100. How much change will she get if she presented a note worth $50 for buying 3 pairs of gloves at the same cost?

Answer: ____________________

(c) Three candles of length 5.13 cm, 2.48 cm and 0.67 cm were joined end to end. Find the total length of the candle thus formed.

Answer: ____________________

(d) The sum of two numbers is 100. If one of them is 62.49, find the other number.

Answer: ____________________

(e) Sophie spent $46.48 on a mat and $13.19 on a jar. How much money did she spent in all?

Answer: ____________________

Integers

1. Solve the following integers.

(a) (–7) + (4) = ☐

(b) (–4) – (–8) = ☐

(c) (–6) – (–6) = ☐

(d) (–18) – (7) = ☐

(e) (10) + (–3) = ☐

(f) (19) – (–4) = ☐

(g) (–5) – (6) = ☐

(h) (–11) – (8) = ☐

(i) (–14) + (2) = ☐

(j) (3) + (–20) = ☐

(k) (16) – (–13) = ☐

(l) (–4) – (12) = ☐

2. Solve the following and write the answer in the given space.

(a) (–8) × (15) = ☐

(b) 72 ÷ (–9) = ☐

(c) (–11) × (–12) = ☐

(d) (–100) ÷ (–10) = ☐

(e) (9) × (–6) = ☐

(f) (–136) ÷ (4) = ☐

(g) (–4) × (–14) = ☐

(h) (75) ÷ (–5) = ☐

(i) (–12) × (10) = ☐

(j) (–400) ÷ (–8) = ☐

(k) (25) × (–8) = ☐

(l) (–208) ÷ (16) = ☐

3. Use BODMAS and solve the following number problems.

(a) $[(-4) \times 5] + [(-8) \div 2]$ = ☐

(b) $[(-18) \div (-3)] + [(-4) \times (-6)]$ = ☐

(c) $[(-9) + 13] \times [8 \div (-2)]$ = ☐

(d) $24 - 4 + [5 \div (-5)]$ = ☐

(e) $[42 \div 7] \times (2 - 8)$ = ☐

(f) $(7 \times 2) - (-2 + 3) + 6$ = ☐

(g) $(-2 \times 3) + (-3 + 6 \div 2)$ = ☐

(h) $(-35 - 5) \div (-2 \times 2)$ = ☐

4. Few workers were digging a well. The well should be 8 metres below the surface. Every day, the workers dig 0.5 m. How many days will they take to complete digging the well?

Ratio

1. Express the ratio in the simplest form.

(a) 125 : 275

(b) 16 : 640

(c) 40 : 56

(d) 27 : 123

(e) 510 : 9

(f) 40 : 100

(g) 21 : 42

(h) 12 : 96

2. Simplify the following ratios.

(a) 800 ml : 4 l

(b) 45 min : 2 hours

(c) 640 g : 3 kg

(d) 1 year : 15 days

(e) 3 hours : 30 minutes

(f) 4 km : 75 m

(g) 15 pencils : 2 dozen pencils

(h) 3 min : 48 seconds

3. Compare the ratios using the signs > , < or =.

(a) 2 : 10 ☐ 4 : 5

(b) 6 : 9 ☐ 11 : 231

(c) 15 : 45 ☐ 12 : 36

(d) 1 : 4 ☐ 28 : 98

(e) 7 : 8 ☐ 4 : 6

(f) 3 : 4 ☐ 5 : 6

(g) 5 : 14 ☐ 9 : 35

(h) 11 : 5 ☐ 3 : 10

4. Find the value of x in the following proportions.

(a) 6 : 15 :: $\boxed{x}$: 60

(b) $\boxed{x}$: 10 :: 8 : 5

(c) 1 : 4 :: 50 : $\boxed{x}$

(d) $\boxed{x}$: 15 :: 8 : 5

(e) 5 : 4 :: $\boxed{x}$: 16

(f) $1 : 5 :: 9 : \boxed{x}$

(g) $9 : 13 :: \boxed{x} : 52$

(h) $12 : \boxed{x} :: 3 : 7$

5. Fill in the blanks given below.

(a) If p : q is a given ratio, p and q are called the ____________ of the ratio.

(b) ____________ and ____________ terms of a proportion are called the extreme terms. (If proportion is p : q :: r : t)

(c) An equality of two ratios is called a ______________.

(d) ____________ and ____________ terms of a proportion are called the mean terms. (If proportion is a : b :: c : d)

(e) If four numbers are in a proportion then the product of ____________ is equal to the product of ____________.

(f) The first term of a ratio is called ____________ and the second term is called ____________.

(g) If a : b :: c : d , then ad = ____________.

(h) If a : b :: b : c , then ac = ____________.

6. Circle the ratios equivalent to the given ratio.

(a)	$\frac{2}{7}$	$\frac{23}{98}$	$\frac{30}{105}$	$\frac{26}{91}$	$\frac{24}{42}$	$\frac{22}{77}$
(b)	$\frac{3}{8}$	$\frac{42}{84}$	$\frac{57}{152}$	$\frac{30}{84}$	$\frac{21}{56}$	$\frac{15}{40}$
(c)	$\frac{4}{5}$	$\frac{32}{40}$	$\frac{84}{115}$	$\frac{68}{94}$	$\frac{100}{125}$	$\frac{13}{17}$
(d)	$\frac{1}{6}$	$\frac{19}{96}$	$\frac{15}{95}$	$\frac{13}{78}$	$\frac{12}{60}$	$\frac{11}{66}$
(e)	$\frac{3}{4}$	$\frac{9}{12}$	$\frac{14}{20}$	$\frac{36}{48}$	$\frac{20}{15}$	$\frac{27}{36}$

7. Solve the following word problems.

Working Space

(a) If 12 girls are wearing 288 bangles, how many bangles will be required for 15 girls assuming that every girl is wearing the same number of bangles.

Answer: ____________________

(b) 435 cookies are packed in 3 cartons. How many cartons are required to pack 1450 cookies?

Answer: ____________________

(c) In a school, there are 275 boys and 225 girls.

Find the ratio of:

(i) the boys to the total number of students. ________________

(ii) the girls to the total number of students. ________________

(iii) the girls to that of boys. ______

(d) Three boys A, B and C collected 360 marbles in the ratio 1:5:3. Find the total number of marbles B has with him.

Answer: ________________

(e) The three angles of a triangle are in the ratio 2:1:2. Find the measurement of the smallest angle of the triangle.

Answer: ________________

Algebra

1. Use signs and symbols to write the following.

(a) Two-third of a number x added to another number y. ____________

(b) Seven less than 12 times a number x. ____________

(c) The product of two numbers y and z subtracted from number x. ________

(d) $3 \times x \times x \times 2 \times x + b \times 5$ ____________

(e) $p \times p \times q \times q \times r \times r + p \times q \times r$ ____________

(f) Five more than 6 times the product of the numbers a and b is __________

2. Identify and write the coefficient of x and y.

Equation	Coefficient of x	Coefficient of y
(a) $4x + 5y + 9 = 2$		
(b) $5ax - 8by - 3 = 7$		
(c) $6px + 3qy = 11$		
(d) $3x - 7y = 15$		
(e) $4by + ax = 3$		
(f) $7x - 3y = 8$		

3. Write the following algebraic expressions in words.

(a) $5x + 9$ ________________________

(b) $\frac{1}{2}d - 7$ ________________________

(c) $y + 3z$ ________________________

(d) $(p + r) + 3s$ ________________________

(e) $10 - 5x$ ________________________

(f) $(a + b) - 12$ ________________________

4. Write down the terms and factors of the following expressions using the tree diagram.

(a) $12x^2 + 18xy + 9$	(b) $ax^2 + bx + c$
(c) $5p + 4q + 7$	(d) $3x^2 + 8x + 5$

5. Evaluate the following.

(a) $a + 2b + 3c$ (where $a = 7, b = 3$ and $c = 2$)

(b) $4a^2 + 3b + 12$ (where $a = 2$ and $b = 5$)

(c) $3x + 8y - 10$ (where $x = 11$ and $y = 6$)

(d) $5xy + y - 3$ (where $x = 3$, and $y = 1$)

Variable Equations

1. Solve the following equations and find the value of the variable in each.

(a) $5x + 6 = 16$

(b) $6y = 84$

(c) $7 + 2x = 15$

(d) $2m = 38$

(e) $3p - 14 = p + 10$

(f) $b - 5 = 6$

2. Write the following equations into statements.

(a) $3m - 6 = 15$ = ______________________

(b) $4y + 10 = 50$ = ______________________

(c) $2x - 16 = 0$ = ______________________

(d) $12y - x = 3$ = ______________________

(e) $2(x + y) = 9$ = ______________________

(f) $t \div 3 = 5$ = ______________________

3. **Solve the following word problems using equations.**

Working Space

(a) The sum of 3 consecutive numbers is 54. Find the three numbers.

Answer: ____________________

(b) When 7 is added to 4 times a number, the result is 87. Find out the number.

Answer: ____________________

(c) A man is four times older than his son. If the sum of their ages is 85, what is the age of the man?

Answer: ____________________

(d) The length of a rectangle is twice its breadth. If the perimeter of the rectangle is 60 m, find its area.

Answer: ____________________

(e) Five more than three times a number is 53. Find the number.

Answer: ____________________

(f) The cost of 5 bags is $105. What is the cost of 2 bags?

Answer: ____________________

(g) 12 more than 3 times a number p is 39. Find the value of p.

Answer: ____________________

(h) A number divided by 3 and increased by 10 gives 14 as the answer. Find the number.

Answer: ____________________

Factors and Multiples

1. Write all the factors of the following numbers.

(a) 57 ____________ (b) 35 ____________

(c) 48 ____________ (d) 55 ____________

(e) 60 ____________ (f) 72 ____________

(g) 100 ____________ (h) 18 ____________

2. Write the first three multiples of the following numbers.

(a) 11 ____________ (b) 7 ____________

(c) 18 ____________ (d) 100 ____________

(e) 25 ____________ (f) 14 ____________

(g) 13 ____________ (h) 20 ____________

3. Fill in the blanks.

(a) ________ is a factor of every number.

(b) The ________ of a number are finite.

(c) There are infinite ________ of a number.

(d) The fifth multiple of 41 is ________.

(e) The prime numbers which differ by 2 are called ________.

(f) The prime factorization of 30 is ________.

(g) The number ________ is neither prime nor composite.

(h) Product of two numbers is always equal to the product of their ________ and ________ .

4. Express the following numbers as the sum of three odd prime numbers.

(a) 29 ________________ (b) 39 ________________

(c) 55 ________________ (d) 43 ________________

5. Write all the multiples of 6 that lie between:

(a) 7 and 30 ________________________________

(b) 50 and 70 ________________________________

6. Write all the multiples of 11 that lie between:

(a) 0 and 60 ________________________________

(b) 100 and 150 ________________________________

7. Write all the pairs of twin primes which are less than 30.

____

8. Use the prime factorization method to find the LCM and HCF of the following numbers.

(a) 25 and 45

(b) 14 and 58

Practice Test 1

1. Evaluate the following.

(a) $(0.4)^3$ = ____________________

(b) $0.5 + \sqrt{169}$ = ____________________

(c) $(0.6)^2 + 1.4$ = ____________________

(d) $(0.2)^2 + 4.8$ = ____________________

(e) $\sqrt{1.44}$ = ____________________

(f) $(2 + 0.2)^2 - 4$ = ____________________

(g) $\sqrt{0.09}$ = ____________________

(h) $[(2 \times 2) - 1.5)] + (0.2)^2$ = ________

2. Simplify the following ratios.

(a) 25 : 175 ⟶ ☐ : ☐

(b) 32 : 88 ⟶ ☐ : ☐

(c) 15025 : 75 ⟶ ☐ : ☐

(d) 25 : 350 ⟶ ☐ : ☐

(e) 42 : 35 ⟶ ☐ : ☐

3. Solve the variable equations.

(a)

$$\begin{array}{r} 3a^2 + 4a - 2 \\ +\quad 2a^2 + 6a + 7 \\ \hline \\ \hline \end{array}$$

(b)

$$\begin{array}{r} 6a^2 - 7a - 2 \\ -\quad a^2 - 2a + 6 \\ \hline \\ \hline \end{array}$$

(c) $\begin{array}{r} 7a^2 - 8a + 2 \\ -\quad 3a^2 + 2a - 6 \\ \hline \\ \hline \end{array}$

(d) $\begin{array}{r} 12a^2 + 4a + 6 \\ -\quad 9a^2 + 3a - 3 \\ \hline \\ \hline \end{array}$

4. Solve the following equations and find the value of x.

(a) $7x - 4 = 24$

(b) $6x + 2 = 4x + 8$

(c) $21x - 2 = 19$

(d) $\frac{x}{3} = 8 + 46$

(e) $5x - 8 = (49 \div 7)$

(f) $\frac{x}{10} = (0.8 \div 0.4)$

5. Solve the following fractions and reduce them to their simplest form.

(a) $\frac{1}{4} + \frac{3}{7} + \frac{2}{7}$

(b) $\frac{5}{8} - (\frac{1}{3} + \frac{1}{6})$

(c) $\frac{8}{15} - \frac{2}{5}$

Percentage

1. Convert the following into per cent by multiplying with 100.

a. $\frac{3}{5}$

b. 0.63

c. $\frac{39}{100}$

d. $3\frac{7}{20}$

e. 1.48

2. Find an equivalent fraction with denominator 100 and then convert into per cent.

a. $\frac{1}{4}$

b. $\frac{6}{25}$

c. $\frac{3}{10}$

d. $\frac{41}{50}$

3. **Write the shaded part of the following as per cent.**

a.

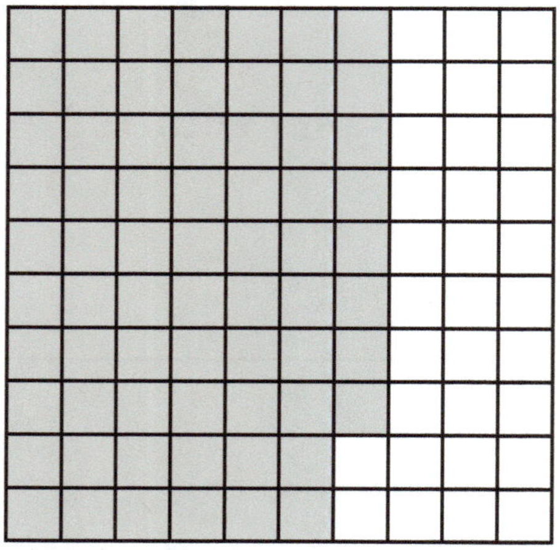

______ %

b.

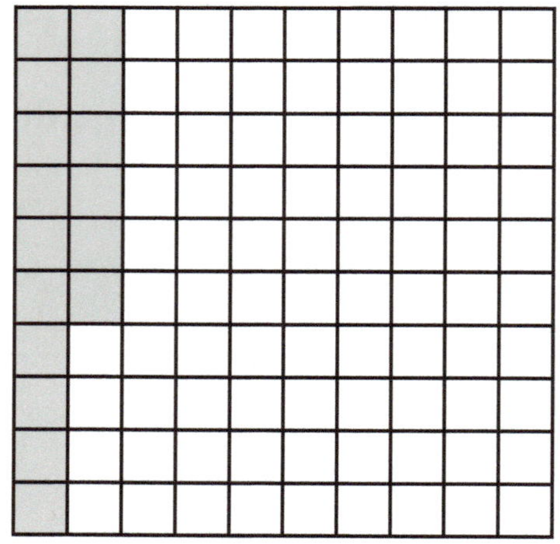

______ %

c.

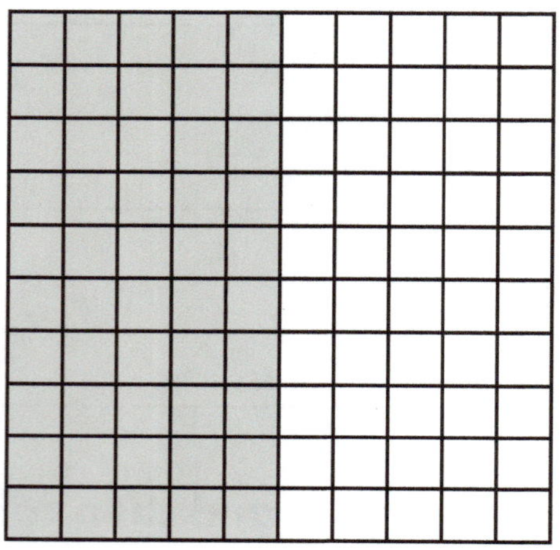

______ %

d.

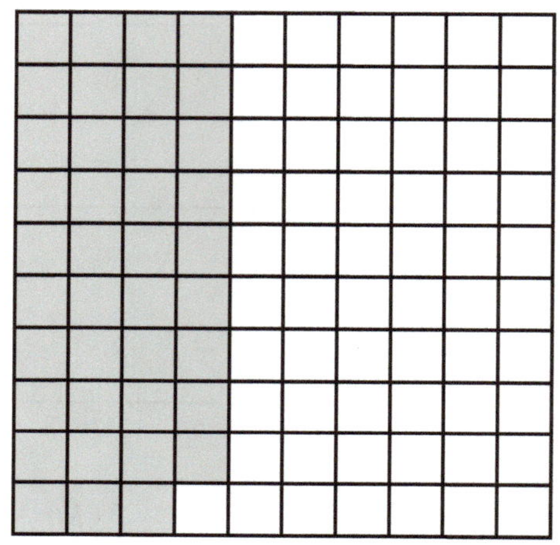

______ %

4. **Convert the following per cent into decimal.**

a. 175% = ______

b. 205 % = ______

c. $\frac{1}{5}$ % = ______

d. 10% = ______

e. $\frac{2}{5}$ % = ______

f. $\frac{4}{5}$ % = ______

g. $1\frac{15}{25}$ % = ______

h. $3\frac{1}{5}$ % = ______

5. Solve the following.

a. 10% of 1 km = ____________________

b. 50% of $20 = ____________________

c. 25% of 4 l = ____________________

d. 5% of 80 mangoes = ____________________

e. 20% of 50 cupcakes = ____________________

6. Read the word problems and answer them.

Working Space

a. Sparsh covers 50% of the distance from his house to the library in a taxi and covers the rest 4 km on foot. How far is the library from his house?

____

b. Saira is reading a book of 200 pages. If she reads 10 pages daily, what per cent of the book will she read in 5 days?

____

c. A fruitseller sold 50% of the fruits in the first half of the day. If he is left with 20 fruits after selling 60 more fruits in the second half of the day, how many fruits did he have in the beginning of the day?

d. Mandy's teacher gave her 12 pages as homework. She completed 25% of them and left the others. How many pages are still there to be done by her?

____

Handling Money

1. Complete the table given below.

Object	Cost price	Selling price	Profit or loss	Profit or loss %
a. Caps	$20	$25	$5 profit	25%
b. Flag	$8	$12	________	________
c. Clock	$15	________	$5 profit	________
d. Bag	$340	________	$20 loss	________
e. Shoes	________	$154	$7 profit	________
f. Socks	________	$38	$4 loss	________
g. Brush	$6	________	$3 profit	________
h. Dress	$120	$150	________	________
i. Shirt	$64	________	$2 loss	________

Working Space

2. Calculate the answer for the following money problems.

(a) Mr. Smith bought a house for $7,50,000. He spent $50,000 on painting it and sold it for $10,00,000. What is the profit percentage?

Answer: ____________________

(b) A lady took an education loan of $60,000 for 6 years at the rate of 11% per annum. How much money will she pay after 6 years with interest?

Answer: ____________________

(c) Find the simple interest and the amount to be paid on a loan of $3,50,000 at 8% per annum for a period of 4 years.

Answer: ____________________

(d) A mobile bill charged $7,180 for the month of June. In the next month, the bill amount was increased by 20%. Calculate the bill for the month of July.

Answer: ____________________

(e) A game whose cost price was $600 was sold at 1.5 times its cost price. What is the profit percentage?

Answer: ____________________

Working Space

Geometrical Concepts

1. Give examples from your daily life that resemble the following.

(a) Curved surface ______________________

(b) Linear boundary ______________________

(c) Plane ______________________

(d) Curved boundary ______________________

(e) Ray ______________________

(f) Line segment ______________________

(g) Angle ______________________

(h) Sector of a circle ______________________

2. Each of the given questions contain a figure. Study the figure and answer the problems.

A. 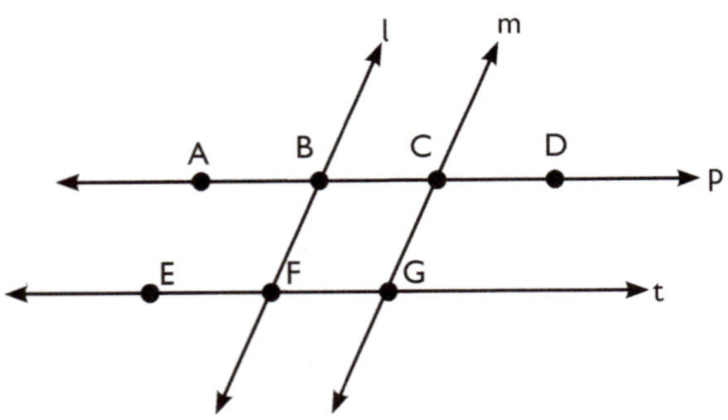

(a) Name three collinear points. _____

(b) Name two lines which are parallel. _____

(c) Name two pairs of intersecting lines. _____

(d) Two rays. _____

(e) Two line segments. _____

B. 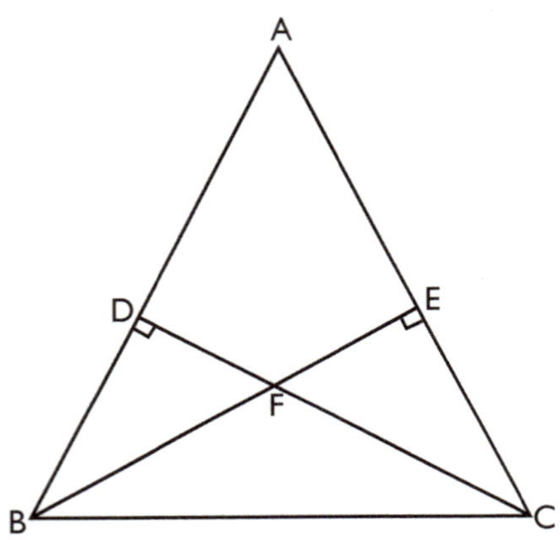

(a) Two right angled triangles. _____

(b) Name 2 altitudes of triangle ABC. _____

(c) Name 2 obtuse angles. _____

(d) Name 2 acute angles. _____

(e) Name a pair of intersecting lines. __________

C.

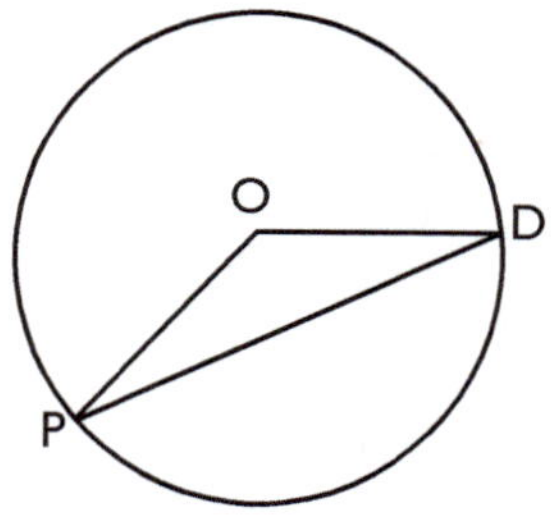

(a) Name any one arc of the circle. _____

(b) Name 2 radii of the circle. _____

(c) Name the minor sector of the circle. _____

(d) Name the major segment of the circle. _____

(e) Name a chord of the circle. _____

3. Answer the following.

(a) How many lines can be drawn through a single point? _____

(b) How many lines can be drawn passing through two points? _____

(c) Three points are plotted on a single line. How many more lines can be drawn through those three collinear points? _____

(d) All the four angles of a quadrilateral are equal. What is the measure of each angle? _____

(e) The boundary of a circle is known as _____.

(f) All radii of a circle are _____ in length.

(g) The longest chord of a circle is also its _____.

(h) There are _____ radii in a circle.

4. Find the measurement of the angle 'x' in the following figures.

(a)

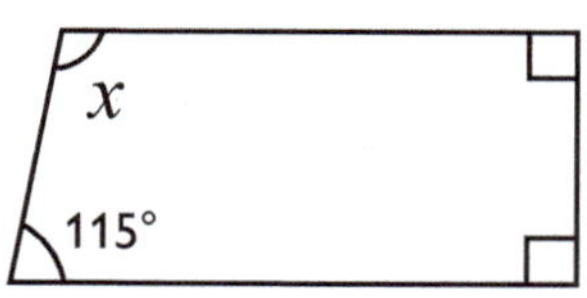

x = ___________

(b)

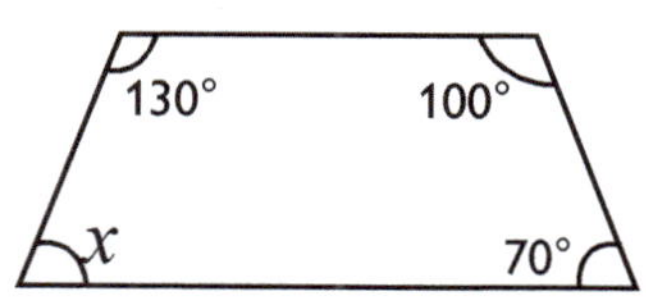

x = ___________

(c)

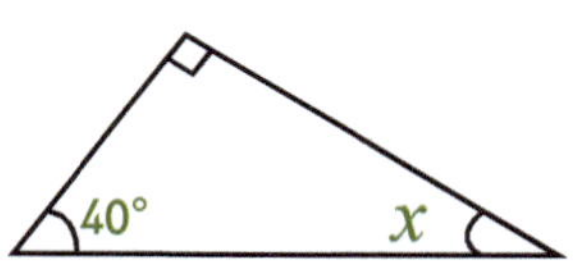

x = ___________

(d)

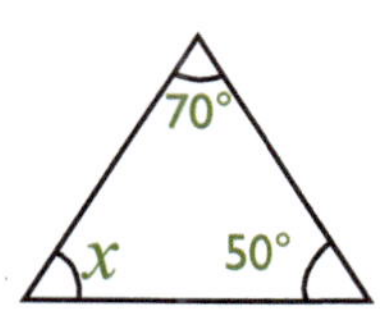

x = ___________

(e)

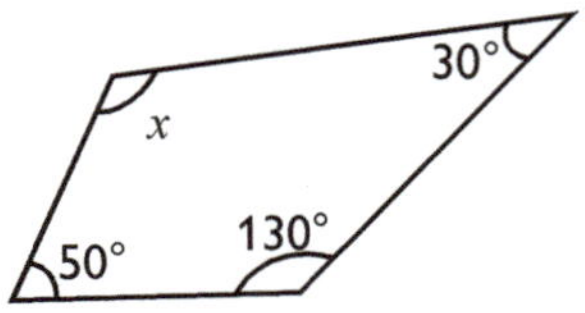

$x =$ ____________

(f)

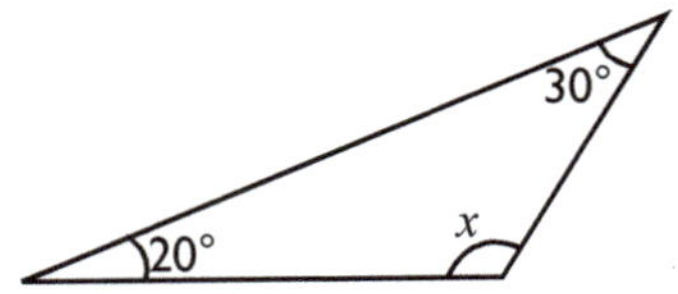

$x =$ ____________

(g)

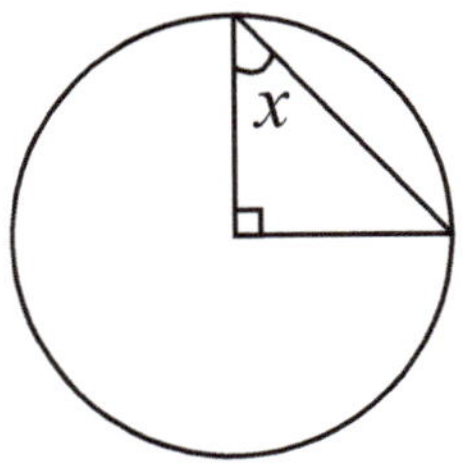

$x =$ ____________

(h)

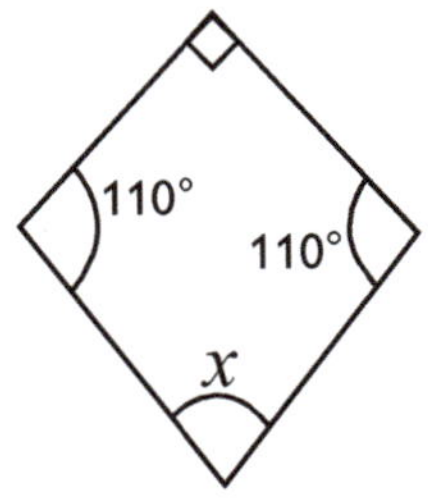

$x =$ ____________

(i)

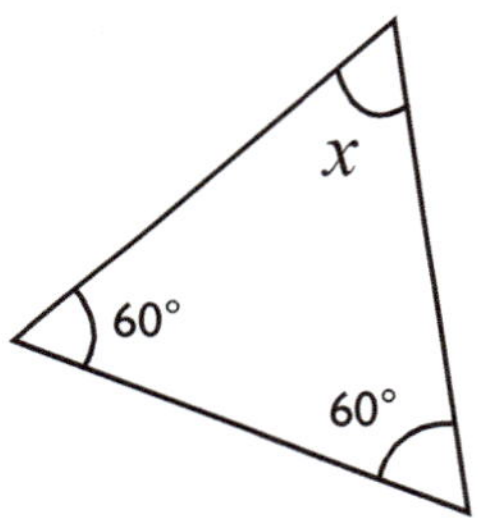

$x =$ ____________

(j)

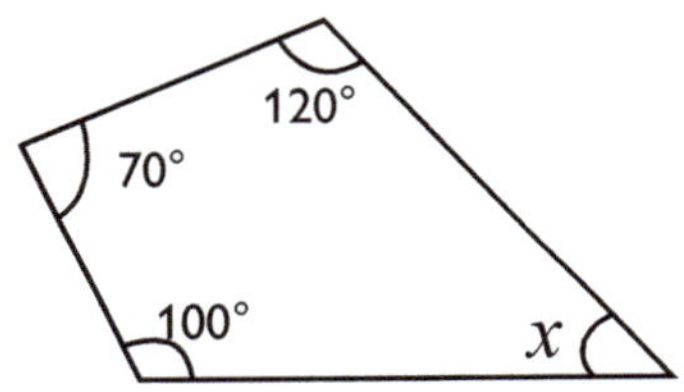

$x =$ ____________

Angles

A. Look at the figures and answer the following.

1. 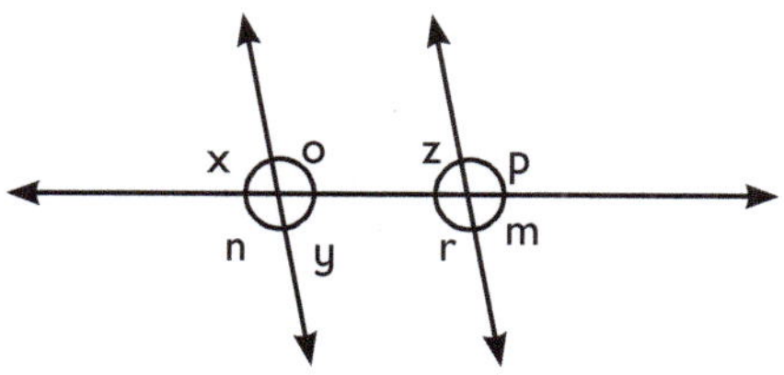

(a) ∠ x = ☐

(b) ∠ n = ☐

(c) ∠ z = ☐ = ☐

(d) ∠ p = ☐ = ☐

(e) ∠ n is corresponding to ☐

(f) ∠ z is vertically opposite to ☐

B. Find the measurement of the following angles.

1. 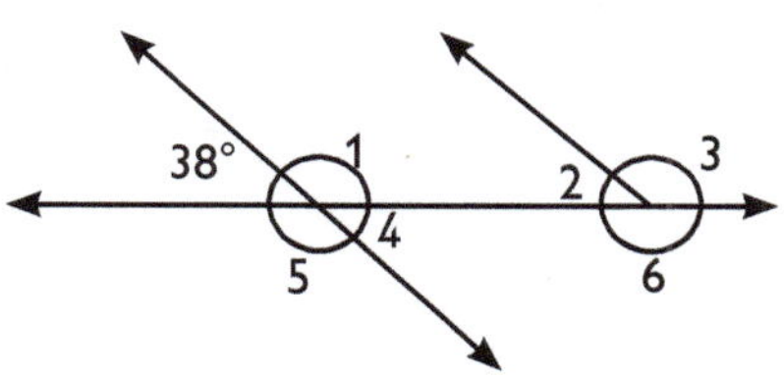

(a) ∠ 1 = ☐

(b) ∠ 2 = ☐

(c) ∠ 3 = ☐

(d) ∠ 4 = ☐

(e) ∠ 5 = ☐

(f) ∠ 6 = ☐

2.

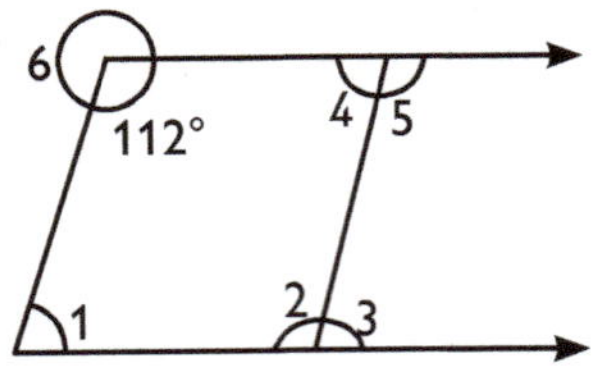

(a) ∠ 1 = ☐

(d) ∠ 4 = ☐

(b) ∠ 2 = ☐

(e) ∠ 5 = ☐

(c) ∠ 3 = ☐

(f) ∠ 6 = ☐

3.

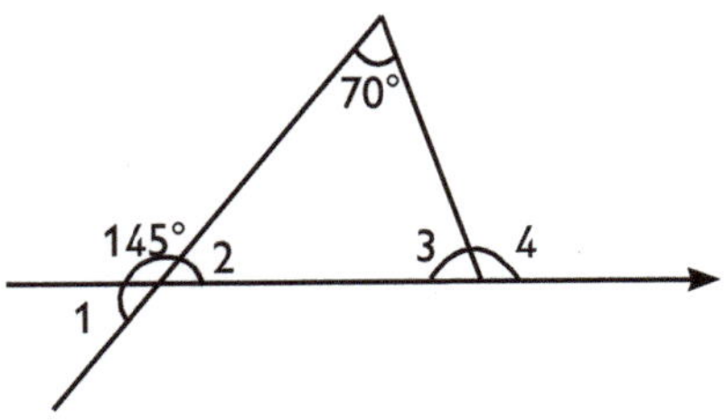

(a) ∠ 1 = ☐

(c) ∠ 3 = ☐

(b) ∠ 2 = ☐

(d) ∠ 4 = ☐

4.

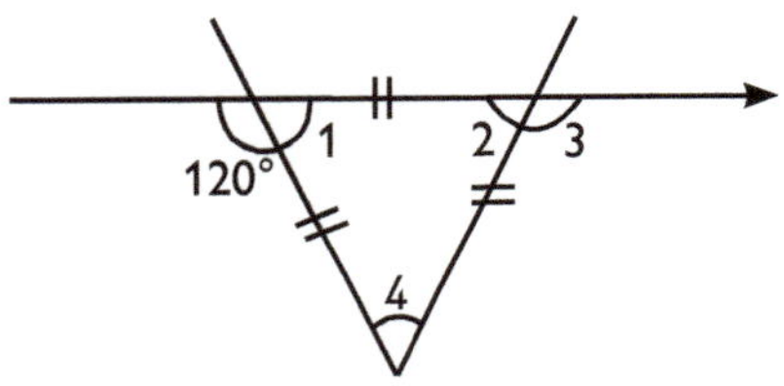

(a) ∠ 1 = ☐

(c) ∠ 3 = ☐

(b) ∠ 2 = ☐

(d) ∠ 4 = ☐

C. Find the measurement of the angle formed between the two hands of a clock at the given time.

(a) 9:00 ____________________

(b) 1:30 ____________________

(c) 12:00 ____________________

(d) 6:00 ____________________

(e) 3:35 ____________________

(f) 8:10 ____________________

(g) 12:20 ____________________

(h) 2:00 ____________________

D. Observe the given figures and classify the angles as acute, obtuse, straight or right angle.

(1)

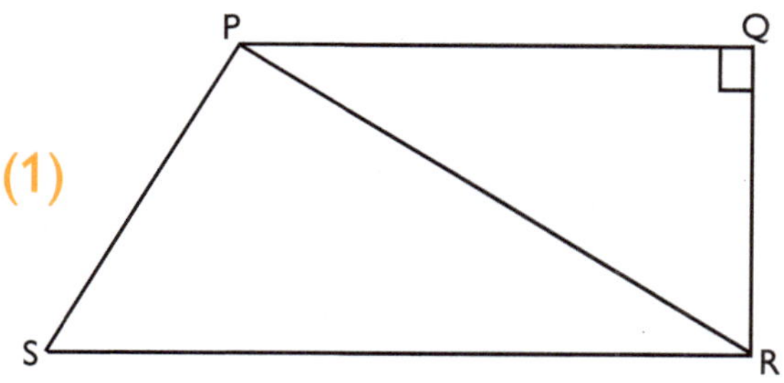

(a) ∠ PSR = ____________

(b) ∠ PQR = ____________

(c) ∠ SPQ = ____________

(d) ∠ PRS = ____________

(e) ∠ SPR = ____________

(2)

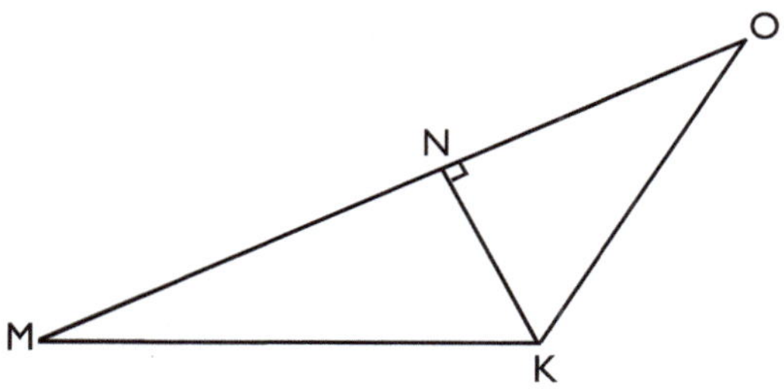

(a) ∠ MKO = ____________

(b) ∠ NMK = ____________

(c) ∠ KNM = ____________

(d) ∠ MOK = ____________

(e) ∠ MNO = ____________

(3)

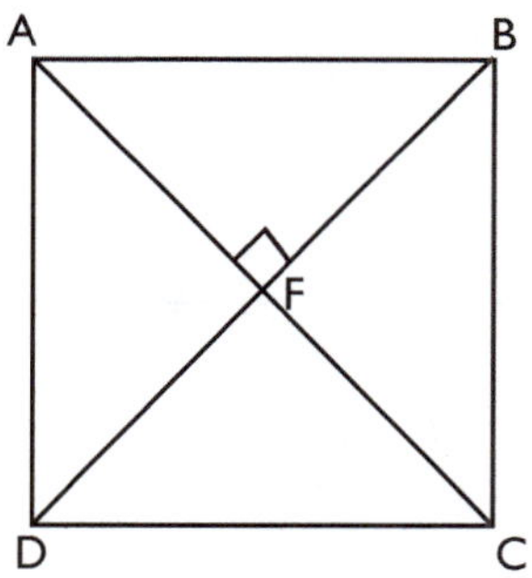

(a) ∠ ACD = ____________

(b) ∠ BCD = ____________

(c) ∠ DFA = ____________

(d) ∠ BDA = ____________

(e) ∠ AFC = ____________

E. Define the following terms.

(a) Line ____________

(b) Ray ____________

(c) Line segment ____________

(d) Polygon ____________

(e) Quadrilateral ____________

(f) Angle ______________________________

(g) Radius ______________________________

(h) Circumference ______________________________

(i) Segment of a circle ______________________________

(j) Sector of a circle ______________________________

F. Find the angles of the following polygons.

(a) The angles of a triangle are in the ratio 1:1:4. Find the measurement of all the angles of the triangle.

(b) Two angles of a quadrilateral are 70° and 90°. If the other two angles are in the ratio 2:3, measure the angles.

Answers

Numbers

1. (a) Seventy eight lakh forty eight thousand three hundred five
   (b) Two crore seven lakh seventy thousand nine hundred ninety nine
   (c) Eighty nine lakh sixty five thousand one hundred thirty
   (d) Seventy three lakh forty nine thousand fifty six
   (e) Four crore thirteen lakh seventy six thousand eight
2. (a) 1,56,530 < 6,56,532 < 7,22,346 < 9,06,490
   (b) 80,009 < 7,81,045 < 9,99,999 < 59,28,640
3. (a) 83,12,756 > 24,88,642 > 6,84,219 > 79,999
   (b) 9,83,651 > 6,53,891 > 5,16,389 > 1,85,963
4. (a) 8000000 + 400000 + 70000 + 6000 + 500 + 30 + 5
   (b) 4000000 + 1000 + 800 + 7
   (c) 20000000+7000000+700000+20000+9000+300+70+2
   (d) 70000000+6000000+900000+60000+40+5
   (e) 10000000+4000000+600000+70000+7000+600+20
5. (a) 3,56,00,373 (b) 49,32,750
   (c) 65,94,00,909 (d) 13,05,00,078
   (e) 70,59,012
6.

(a)	7,69,148	7,71,148
(b)	40,40,400	40,50,500
(c)	47,11,497	57,11,497
(d)	8,53,651	8,54,661
(e)	54,785	55,285

7. (a) 5000 (b) 19000 (c) 24000
   (d) 36000 (e) 20000 (f) 100000
   (g) 183000 (h) 259000
8. (a) 11000, 10874 (b) 90000, 89579
   (c) 35000, 34795 (d) 15000, 14820
   (e) 4000, 4050 (f) 5000, 4600
   (g) 173000, 172800
9. (a) 400 (b) 500 (c) 600
   (d) 1100 (e) 200 (f) 1100
   (g) 800 (h) 1000
10. (a) 1654 (b) 157 (c) 74
    (d) 68 (e) 1250 (f) 960
    (g) 706 (h) 1105
11. (a) $15648 (b) 14000 balls
    (c) 8,00,000 words (d) 21,85,000 votes

Number Operations

1. (a) 15761 (b) 688 (c) 18096
   (d) 564170 (e) 1221 (f) 34375
   (g) 7091449 (h) 4325 (i) 679712
   (j) 51837
2. (a) 43 (b) 6 (c) 105
   (d) 800
3. (a) 55 (b) BODMAS (c) 16
   (d) 14

Fractions

1. (a) $\frac{5}{6}$ (b) $\frac{10}{3}$ (c) $\frac{4}{5}$
   (d) $\frac{5}{6}$ (e) $\frac{3}{4}$ (f) $\frac{8}{25}$
2. (a) $\frac{10}{26}, \frac{15}{39}, \frac{20}{52}$ (b) $\frac{8}{14}, \frac{12}{21}, \frac{16}{28}$
   (c) $\frac{1}{2}, \frac{18}{36}, \frac{27}{54}$ (d) $\frac{10}{16}, \frac{15}{24}, \frac{20}{32}$
   (e) $\frac{4}{22}, \frac{6}{33}, \frac{8}{44}$ (f) $\frac{14}{18}, \frac{21}{27}, \frac{28}{36}$
3. (a) $\frac{24}{88} = \frac{15}{55} = \frac{51}{187} = \frac{33}{121}$
   (b) $\frac{36}{78} = \frac{54}{117} = \frac{66}{143} = \frac{78}{169}$
   (c) $\frac{55}{88} = \frac{60}{96} = \frac{75}{120} = \frac{100}{160}$
   (d) $\frac{24}{108} = \frac{18}{81} = \frac{56}{252} = \frac{24}{108}$
   (e) $\frac{60}{105} = \frac{72}{126} = \frac{52}{91} = \frac{400}{700}$
4. (a) = (b) > (c) < (d) <
   (e) < (f) > (g) < (h) <
5. (a) $\frac{1}{7}, \frac{4}{14}, \frac{3}{7}, \frac{6}{7}, \frac{9}{7}$
   (b) $\frac{1}{9}, \frac{2}{7}, \frac{4}{7}, \frac{3}{5}, \frac{4}{5}$
   (c) $\frac{2}{12}, \frac{3}{12}, \frac{4}{12}, \frac{6}{12}$
   (d) $\frac{5}{8}, \frac{2}{3}, \frac{3}{4}, \frac{8}{9}$

6. (a) $\frac{3}{6}, \frac{4}{9}, \frac{1}{3}, \frac{1}{8}$
   (b) $\frac{15}{11}, \frac{9}{11}, \frac{7}{11}, \frac{5}{11}, \frac{2}{11}$
   (c) $\frac{8}{13}, \frac{6}{15}, \frac{3}{13}, \frac{1}{15}$
   (d) $\frac{5}{6}, \frac{2}{3}, \frac{1}{2}, \frac{1}{4}$

7. (a) $\frac{146}{91}$ (b) $\frac{266}{45}$ (c) $\frac{1}{3}$
   (d) $\frac{79}{15}$ (e) $\frac{347}{48}$ (f) $\frac{32}{45}$

8. (a) unit (b) like (c) inverse
   (d) $\frac{39}{8}$ (e) unlike (f) $\frac{6}{34}$
   (g) $\frac{1}{4}$

9. (a) $3\frac{3}{4}$ m (b) 3 cups
   (c) 245 pages (d) 16.425 grams
   (e) 9.6 m (f) $5\frac{1}{2}$ litres

Decimals

1. (a) 0.6 (b) 15.9 (c) 5.6
   (d) 9.1 (e) 7.02 (f) 0.675
   (g) 0.25 (h) 7.02 (i) 9
   (j) 10

2. (a) Hundredths (b) Tens
   (c) Thousandths (d) Tenths

3. (a) 1.3 (b) 0.936 (c) 0.52
   (d) 8.3 (e) 0.07 (f) 1
   (g) 4

4. (a) 44.8 m (b) $12.50 (c) 8.28 cm
   (d) 37.51 (e) $59.67

Integers

1. (a) –3 (b) 4 (c) 0
   (d) –25 (e) 7 (f) 23
   (g) –11 (h) –19 (i) –12
   (j) –17 (k) 29 (l) –16

2. (a) –120 (b) –8 (c) 132
   (d) 10 (e) –54 (f) –34
   (g) 56 (h) –15 (i) –120
   (j) 50 (k) –200 (l) –13

3. (a) –24 (b) 30 (c) –16
   (d) 19 (e) –36 (f) 19
   (g) –6 (h) 10

4. 16 days

Ratio

1. (a) 5:11 (b) 1:40 (c) 5:7
   (d) 9:41 (e) 170:3 (f) 2:5
   (g) 1:2 (h) 1:8

2. (a) 1:5 (b) 3:8 (c) 16:75
   (d) 73:3 (e) 6:1 (f) 160:3
   (g) 5:8 (h) 15:4

3. (a) $<$ (b) $>$ (c) =
   (d) $<$ (e) $>$ (f) $<$
   (g) $>$ (h) $>$

4. (a) $x = 24$ (b) $x = 16$ (c) $x = 200$
   (d) $x = 24$ (e) $x = 20$ (f) $x = 45$
   (g) $x = 36$ (h) $x = 28$

5. (a) terms (b) p and t
   (c) proportion (d) b and c
   (e) means, extremes
   (f) antecedent, consequent
   (g) b × c (h) b^2

6. (a) $\frac{30}{105}, \frac{26}{91}, \frac{22}{77}$ (b) $\frac{57}{152}, \frac{21}{56}, \frac{15}{40}$
   (c) $\frac{32}{40}, \frac{100}{125}$ (d) $\frac{13}{78}, \frac{11}{66}$
   (e) $\frac{9}{12}, \frac{36}{48}, \frac{27}{36}$

7. (a) 360 bangles (b) 10 cartons
   (c) (i) 11:20 (ii) 9:20 (iii) 9:11
   (d) 200 marbles (e) 36°

Algebra

1. (a) $\frac{2}{3}x + y$ (b) $12x - 7$
   (c) $x - yz$ (d) $6x^3 + 5b$
   (e) $p^2q^2r^2 + pqr$ (f) $6ab + 5$

2. (a) 4, 5 (b) $5a, (-8b)$
   (c) $6p, 3q$ (d) 3, –7
   (e) $4b, a$ (f) 7, –3

3. (a) Nine more than five times a number x.
   (b) Seven less than half of a number d.
   (c) A number y is added to three times a number z.
   (d) Three times a number s is added to the sum of numbers p and r.
   (e) Five times a number x is subtracted from ten.
   (f) Twelve is subtracted from the sum of a and b.

4. (a) $(2\times2\times3\times x\times x) + (2\times3\times3\times x\times y) + (3\times3)$
   (b) $(a \times x \times x) + (b \times x) + (c)$
   (c) $(5 \times p) + (2 \times 2 \times q) + 7$
   (d) $(3 \times x \times x) + (2 \times 2 \times 2 \times x) + 5$
5. (a) 19 (b) 43
   (c) 71 (d) 13

Variable Equations

1. (a) 2 (b) 14 (c) 4
   (d) 19 (e) 12 (f) 11
2. (a) Six less than three times a number is fifteen.
   (b) Ten more than four times a number is fifty.
   (c) Sixteen subtracted from twice a number is zero.
   (d) A number x subtracted from twelve times a number y is three.
   (e) Twice the sum of two numbers x and y is equal to nine.
   (f) A number divided by three is equal to five.
3. (a) 17, 18, 19 (b) 20 (c) 68 years
   (d) 200 m^2 (e) 16 (f) $42
   (g) 9 (h) 12

Factors and Multiples

1. (a) 57 = 1, 3, 19, 57
   (b) 35 = 1, 5, 7, 35
   (c) 48 = 1, 2, 3, 4, 6, 8, 12, 16, 24, 48
   (d) 55 = 1, 5, 11, 55
   (e) 60 = 1, 2, 3, 4, 5, 6, 10, 12, 15, 20, 30 60
   (f) 72 = 1, 2, 3, 4, 6, 8, 9, 12, 18, 36, 72
   (g) 100 = 1, 2, 4, 5, 10, 20, 25, 50, 100
   (h) 18 = 1, 2, 3, 6, 9, 18
2. (a) 11, 22, 33 (b) 7, 14, 21
   (c) 18, 36, 54 (d) 100, 200, 300
   (e) 25, 50, 75 (f) 14, 28, 42
   (g) 13, 26, 39 (h) 20, 40, 60
3. (a) 1 (b) factors (c) multiples
   (d) 205 (e) twin primes (f) 2 × 3 × 5
   (g) 1 (h) LCM and HCF
4. (a) 5 + 13 + 11 (b) 3 + 13 + 23
   (c) 7 + 17 + 31 (d) 7 + 17 + 19
5. (a) 12, 18, 24 (b) 54, 60, 66
6. (a) 11, 22, 33, 44, 55 (b) 110, 121, 132, 143
7. 3 and 5, 5 and 7, 11 and 13, 17 and 19
8. (a) LCM = 225, HCF = 5
   (b) LCM = 406, HCF = 2

Practice Test 1

1. (a) 0.064 (b) 13.5 (c) 1.76
   (d) 4.84 (e) 1.2 (f) 0.84
   (g) 0.3 (h) 2.54
2. (a) 1:7 (b) 4:11 (c) 601:3
   (d) 1:14 (e) 6:5
3. (a) $5a^2 + 10a + 5$ (b) $5a^2 - 5a - 8$
   (c) $4a^2 - 10a + 8$ (d) $3a^2 + a + 9$
4. (a) 4 (b) 3 (c) 1
   (d) 162 (e) 3 (f) 20
5. (a) $\frac{27}{28}$ (b) $\frac{1}{8}$ (c) $\frac{2}{15}$

Percentage

1. (a) 60% (b) 63% (c) 39%
   (d) 335% (e) 148%
2. (a) $\frac{1}{4} = \frac{25}{100} = 25\%$ (b) $\frac{6}{25} = \frac{24}{100} = 24\%$
   (c) $\frac{3}{10} = \frac{30}{100} = 30\%$ (d) $\frac{41}{50} = \frac{82}{100} = 82\%$
3. (a) 68% (b) 16%
   (c) 50% (d) 39%
4. (a) 1.75 (b) 2.05 (c) 0.002
   (d) 0.1 (e) 0.004 (f) 0.008
   (g) 0.016 (h) 0.032
5. (a) 100 m (b) $10 (c) 1 l
   (d) 4 mangoes (e) 10 cupcakes
6. (a) 8 km (b) 25%
   (c) 160 fruits (d) 9 pages

Handling Money

2. (a) 25% profit (b) $99,600
   (c) S.I.=$1,12,000 Amount = $4,62,000
   (d) $8,616 (e) 50%

Geometrical Concepts

1. (a) Ball, Bowl
   (b) The edge of a book
   (c) The flat surface of a table
   (d) The edge of a circular disc
   (e) Ray of light from the sun or a lamp
   (f) Pencil, Edge of a ruler
   (g) Door hinge, Bike spokes
   (h) A slice of pizza

2

A. (a) A, B, C (b) l and m

(c) m and p (d) ray $\overrightarrow{CD}$ and $\overrightarrow{FE}$
(e) $\overleftrightarrow{BC}$ and $\overleftrightarrow{FG}$

B. (a) ΔCBD, ΔBEC (b) CD and BE
(c) ∠DFE, ∠BFC (d) ∠BFD, ∠CFE
(e) DC and BE

C. (a) $\overset{\frown}{PD}$ (b) OD and OP
(c) sector POD (d) segment PD
(e) PD

3. (a) infinite (b) one
(c) 0 (d) 90°
(e) circumference (f) equal
(g) diameter (h) infinite

4. (a) 65° (b) 60° (c) 50°
(d) 60° (e) 150° (f) 130°
(g) 45° (h) 50° (i) 60°
(j) 70°

Angles

A. 1. (a) ∠y (b) ∠o
(c) ∠m, ∠y (d) ∠r = ∠n
(e) ∠r (f) ∠m

B. 1. (a) 142° (b) 38° (c) 142°
(d) 38° (e) 142° (f) 180°
2. (a) 68° (b) 112° (c) 68°
(d) 68° (e) 112° (f) 248°
3. (a) 35° (b) 35° (c) 75°
(d) 105°
4. (a) 60° (b) 60° (c) 120°
(d) 60°

C. (a) 90° (b) 150° (c) 0°
(d) 180° (e) 120° (f) 180°
(g) 120° (h) 60°

D. 1. (a) acute (b) right
(c) obtuse (d) acute
(e) acute
2. (a) obtuse (b) acute
(c) right (d) acute
(e) straight
3. (a) acute (b) right
(c) right (d) acute
(e) straight

F. (a) 30°, 30°, 120° (b) 80°, 120°